A Woop in my Soup

Written By Keith Lawrence Roman

Illustrated By Barbara Litwiniec

A special acknowledgement
Without Dr. Seuss
There would be no Woop!

I wouldn't have minded.
I wouldn't have cared

If he'd have just asked
me politely to share.

But Woops are not like
that, no they are not.

Woops are a selfish and
self-centered lot.

If you have a nickel
He wants a dime.

If you have a watch
He wants all your time.

Whatever you have, he wants it and more.
If you go to sleep, he wants all your snores.

Woops are a greedy and
self-centered lot.

They want from you...

Whatever you've got!

My mother called "dinner" and I
ran to eat
Racing as if I had 12 extra feet.

I was so hungry, the food smelled so great
          Dashing and diving for something to taste.
And in my hurry, and in my haste,
          I laid a few people and objects to waste.

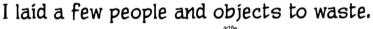

One was my sister, my sister Kate,
          Playing with dolls inside of the gate.
Her tea party ended in smash and debris
          She got in my way, so who could blame me?

Once in the house I tripped on the dog.
Poor little Ralphie slept like a log.
Until my left foot stepped on his tail.
He yelped and he howled and let out a wail.

Last on the list was my
mother's vase,

That crashed on the floor
when I bumped its base.

Accidents happen,
I said to myself,

Just as another vase
fell from the shelf.

Puppies and people and objects of art
Flew by the way as I made a dart.
Too bad for them, for I couldn't wait.
I pushed and I shoved my way to my plate.

Into the kitchen I hurried to eat.
I pulled out my chair and jumped to my seat.

But there at the table, along with the food,
Was something that I found incredibly crude.

Sitting in comfort, resting with ease,
There sat a Woop in my soup made of peas.

I'd seen him before, this hideous beast,
Now sitting relaxing in my supper feast.
They always appear at just about six
Or close to whenever my dinner is fixed.

There on the table, out of control,
Sat a small Woop with his feet in my bowl.
My hands on my face, my eyes in a roll,
I stared at that horrible Woop of a troll.

A Woop is a creature just 12 inches tall.

He's not very big, but not very small.

For Woops have a feature, hidden to see.

Woops have a pair of huge big ugly feet.

Six toes on their right foot,
eight on their left.

They walk round in circles,
off balance at best.

This makes their feet tired,
too heavy to heft.

They slide them in soup
to soothe them and rest.

Woops are all fuzzy except for their peds,
Their eyes, and their nose, and a patch on their heads.

Their faces and bodies are covered with hair.
If not for their clothing, you'd think they were bears.

But unlike a grizzly, Woops like to dress
In surfer dude shorts with sharp matching vests.

They often wear buttons and pins on their clothes
From long past elections and radio shows.

They wear granny glasses that hang on their nose
That let them see closely your highs and your lows.

My dinner was ended, my appetite ceased,
By some type of troll with huge big ugly feet.

Kate and my mother then came through the door.
Their food undisturbed, the Woop they ignored.
The Woop then pretended that they weren't there.
He reached in his pocket and pulled out a chair.

He set up the chair on the edge of my plate
Then leaned back relaxing, content just to wait.
He held in his hand a small paper umbrella
And sitting beneath it this obnoxious fellah.

I called to my mother, I screamed to be heard.
I opened my mouth, but out came no words.
I wanted to say, "There's a Woop in my soup."
But all that came out was some gobbledy goop.

I sputtered and stammered my words all a mess.
Then I decided the Woop to address.
He sat there just smiling, a picture of grace.
I shouted with fury to his furry face.

Suddenly changed, my words came out clear.
Unlike my Mother, my voice he could hear.
"Whatever you want, whatever you need,
Get out of my dinner of soup made of peas."

The Woop then turned towards me and lowered his nose.
He smiled with a sneer and wiggled his toes.
"My feet are tired and they need a rest.
Soup made of peas is the rest they like best."

I looked in his eyes but they showed no fear.
While grinding my teeth I said "Get out of here."
That Woop spoke to me. He spoke right out loud.
"Listen to me and don't act so proud."

"I'll leave when I'm ready and then I'll return,
Whenever I think there's a lesson to learn.
You'd better listen for I won't repeat.
You'll just stay hungry and you'll never eat,
As long as your dinner is cooled by my feet."

"You pushed and shoved your way to this plate.
You stepped on poor Ralphie and knocked over Kate.
Your mother's fine china cannot be repaired.
You thought of yourself, for that's all you cared."

I knew he was right, but what could I say
The damage was done, what price should I pay?

What punishment proper for being a Woop
For putting my own feet in everyone's soup?

I saw that my mother and my sister Kate
Had finished their dinner, had emptied their plates.
With no better time and no better way,
To make wrong things right, to them I did say,
"Let me do the dishes, I'll clear this mess.
Both of you sit on the sofa and rest."

For a dessert my
mother had baked,
Her fabulous three layer
dark chocolate cake.

I was so tempted and I
couldn't wait,
To dig in a fork for
all I could take.

But something inside me then changed my mind.
I had decided to try and be kind.

So then instead I sliced up the sweet
And carried it out to my family to eat.

Then I returned to finish the dishes
To see had been granted one of my wishes.

The Woop was no longer bathed in my food.
Instead he now seemed in a much better mood.

The Woop said to me, "You wash and I'll dry.
Apparently you're not too bad of a guy.
You just need to learn that sharing is best
Or else you'll again have a Woop as a guest."

We finished the dishes and sat down in chairs.
The last piece of chocolate dessert we then shared.

Woops are quite strange, I think you'll agree.
But then they're a lot just like you and like me.

There is a Woop inside of us all.
He's not very big, not twelve inches tall.

Still he arises, still he appears,
And with him we travel our days and our years.

How we treat others, who we take from,
Make who we are now and who we become.

Once in a while, first think of others
Even if they are not sister or brothers.

Treat those you know and everyone else
The way you would like them to be to yourself.

But if you insist on being a goof,
You just might find...

A Woop in your Soup

About The Author

Keith Lawrence Roman has been writing stories of all kinds since he was seven years old. He has written over twenty different children's books, in several different styles.

Keith's favorite books from his childhood were Mike Mulligan and his Steam Shovel, Horton Hears a Who, Harold's Purple Crayon and every book ever written by Beverly Cleary.

His most popular books are rhyming children's picture books like the best-selling I Sat Beside An Elephant.

Yet his personal favorites among his books are young adult novels such as The Midget Green Swamp Moose, fairy tales like The White Handkerchief and chapter books for children 8 years old and up.

Keith was raised in a small town on the North shore of Long Island, New York. He considers himself an original baby boomer and a true child of the 60s.

He vividly remembers standing in snow every winter day, with near frozen toes waiting, for an always late school bus.

Keith takes great pride in that "somehow all those beautiful ideals we believed in from 1968 are still intact within me."

Keith speaks one on one with thousands of children every year and reminds them that, as Dr. Seuss said, "There's nobody youer than you."

His advice for writers both young and old is the same.

"First, make sure you are madly in love with your idea for a story. Much of writing is boring drudgery. Your idea must be strong enough to keep your inspiration alive while you write the story. Second, Do not paint only the branches of the writing tree, paint every leaf with all its color. And finally, don't wait until you are 57 to publish your first book. Let nothing in life frighten or distract you from expressing your thoughts."

Keith currently lives in Orlando, Florida where his feet are never too cold.